P9-DFZ-550

BETHEL PUBLIC LIBRARY
3 4030 03827 6405

Robert Quackenbush

RICKSHAW TO HORROR

A Miss Mallard Mystery

•

Prentice-Hall, Inc.
Englewood Cliffs, New Jersey

Printed in the United States of America •J

Prentice-Hall International, Inc., London
Prentice-Hall of Australia, Pty. Ltd., Sydney
Prentice-Hall Canada, Inc., Toronto
Prentice-Hall of India Private Ltd., New Delhi
Prentice-Hall of Japan, Inc., Tokyo
Prentice-Hall of Southeast Asia Pte. Ltd., Singapore
Whitehall Books Limited, Wellington, New Zealand
Editora Prentice-Hall Do Brasil LTDA., Rio de Janeiro

10 9 8 7 6 5 4 3 2 1

Library of Congress Cataloging in Publication Data

Quackenbush, Robert M.
Rickshaw to horror.

Summary: Miss Mallard, the world-famous duck detective, visits Hong Kong, where she encounters a retired English military duck who seems to have the power to predict disasters.
[1. Mystery and detective stories. 2. Ducks—Fiction. 3. Hong Kong—Fiction. 4. Extrasensory perception—Fiction] I. Title.
PZ7.Q16Ri 1984 [Fic] 83-19083
ISBN 0-13-781014-8

FOR PIET

All of Hong Kong was celebrating the Dragon Boat Festival. Boat-racing teams had come from all over the world. On one street, a Dragon Dance went weaving back and forth through the crowd. Suddenly, a rickshaw raced ahead of the dragon.

"Lee Long Duck!" cried Miss Mallard, the world-famous ducktective. "Please slow down! You're going much too fast! How can I see the sights of Hong Kong at this speed?"

"Sorry," said Lee Long Duck.

Lee Long Duck quickly turned a corner onto a quieter street. At the same moment, someone stepped off the sidewalk and was knocked down by the rickshaw.

"Horrors!" cried Miss Mallard. "We hit someone!"

Lee Long Duck stopped the rickshaw. Miss Mallard jumped out and looked under it as a police officer came running over.

"Are you all right under there?" called Miss Mallard. "I'm Margery Mallard. I've seen you before. We're staying at the same hotel. I'm terribly sorry about this."

"Marshall Gadwall, retired navy captain, here," quacked a feeble voice. "I'm fine. Just a bit dizzy from hitting my head."

Gadwall crawled out from under the rickshaw. He looked dazed.

"Perhaps you should see a doctor," said the police officer.

"No, no," said Gadwall. "I am quite all right. Besides, this is Sunday and it is nearly eleven o'clock. I must be off to an important appointment."

"But today is Saturday," said Miss Mallard.

"No, Sunday," said Gadwall. "Don't you remember? At this same hour yesterday—Saturday—someone raised a typhoon warning flag at the ferry terminal. All the ferries stopped running and everyone rushed for shelter."

The police officer said, "I'll prove to you that today is Saturday."

He called someone on his walkie-talkie. When he finished, he looked at Gadwall.

"Great Dragons!" he said. "Someone *did* raise a false warning flag at the terminal just now. The crowd is in a panic and the police are trying to sort things out. But how could you predict it? It must be a coincidence. You had better go to your hotel now. I'm Officer Pintail, if you should need me again."

"I'll take Captain Gadwall to the hotel," said Miss Mallard. "It's just around the corner."

At the hotel, Gadwall decided to have some tea. He asked Miss Mallard to join him.

"I never could turn down a cup of tea," said Miss Mallard.

"Good!" said Gadwall. "I'll meet you in the lounge. I must send my valet, Harold, on an errand. My wife, Melissa, is shopping and should return soon. I'd like you two to meet."

Miss Mallard went into the lounge. At a table by the window, she sat down facing the lobby. While she was waiting, she took a travel guidebook from her knitting bag and began to read. The book said that a million-dollar jade necklace was on display at the Duckworth Museum.

"I'd like to see that," she thought.

THINGS TO DO IN HONG KONG!
$1,000,000 JADE NECKLACE

HONG KONG
TRAVEL GUIDE

Miss Mallard looked up and saw Gadwall talking to Harold, who was wearing a gray valet's jacket. Then Harold left, and Mrs. Gadwall came into the hotel. Gadwall brought his wife into the lounge.

"I'm pleased to meet you," said Melissa Gadwall. "Are you here for the Dragon Boat Festival?"

"Yes," said Miss Mallard. "And you?"

"I prefer shopping," said Melissa Gadwall. "Especially for jade."

Marshall Gadwall cleared his throat and changed the subject. He told his wife about the accident.

"And the strangest thing, dear!" Gadwall said. "When I was hit on the head, I could predict things."

"Like what?" asked his wife.

Suddenly, Gadwall turned very silent. He looked at his watch. Then he looked at Miss Mallard.

"What's wrong?" asked Miss Mallard.

"In exactly five minutes," said Gadwall, "it will be twelve o'clock. That's when someone will cut the ropes of the famous Peeking Duck Floating Restaurant and set it adrift in the harbor."

Miss Mallard gasped and got up from the table.

"What is this about?" pleaded Melissa Gadwall.

"It is another of your husband's predictions!" said Miss Mallard. "Wait here. I'll notify the police!"

Miss Mallard ran outside. She saw Lee Long Duck and waved to him. He rushed over with his rickshaw and Miss Mallard climbed in.

"Take me to Officer Pintail!" said Miss Mallard. "And forget what I said before. This time you can hurry!"

They found Officer Pintail on a side street. Miss Mallard told him about the new prediction.

"I'll check it out," said Officer Pintail. "The restaurant is only a few blocks away."

They all rushed to the waterfront. When they got there, the Peeking Duck Floating Restaurant had been cut loose from its ropes. It was drifting out to sea. Everyone on board was quacking loudly to be rescued. Officer Pintail called for help on his walkie-talkie.

In a flash, firetrucks and police cars came racing to the waterfront. At the same time, out in the harbor, rescue boats were at work. They pushed the restaurant back to shore.

When the floating restaurant was safe, Officer Pintail filled out a report. The restaurant manager said that he did not know who cut the ropes. He asked who had sounded the alarm.

"I did," said Miss Mallard.

"I am very grateful to you," said the manager. "Please be our guest for dinner any time."

"Actually," said Miss Mallard, "someone at my hotel, Marshall Gadwall, warned me that you were in danger."

"Please invite him to dinner, too," said the manager.

Miss Mallard said that she would. Then she went looking for Lee Long Duck. On the way, she saw a gray thread dangling from one of the cut ropes of the floating restaurant.

"Hmmmm," she said.

She looked at the thread with her magnifying glass. Then she put it between the pages of her travel guide and put the book back in her knitting bag. Afterward, she found Lee Long Duck and rode away in his rickshaw.

When Miss Mallard at last returned to the hotel, she found Gadwall alone in the lounge. He said that Mrs. Gadwall had gone shopping again. Miss Mallard told him how his second prediction had come true. She also told him about the manager's dinner invitation.

"That was nice of him," said Gadwall. "But I won't be able to go. Floating restaurants make me seasick."

Just then, Officer Pintail arrived. He needed some information for his report on the restaurant. He asked Gadwall how he was able to predict bad events.

"I have no idea," said Gadwall. "Ever since the rickshaw accident, pictures just seem to pop into my head."

Suddenly he stopped talking and looked at his watch. "What is it?" asked Miss Mallard.

Gadwall answered, "In five minutes, it will be exactly three o'clock. That's when someone will let the air out of the tires of all the tour buses at the Victoria Bazaar. There will be a major traffic jam."

Officer Pintail was alarmed.

"Wait here!" he said to Gadwall as he ran from the hotel.

Miss Mallard ran, too. She hired Lee Long Duck to take her to the bazaar. When she got there, she saw all the flat tires and the major traffic jam that Gadwall had described. There were ducks everywhere, nearly quacking their heads off. And just as before, the police could not find out who had done it.

HONG KONG

It was several hours before the tires were fixed and the police unsnarled the traffic. All the while, Miss Mallard kept looking for clues. But she found nothing. Finally, she had Lee Long Duck take her back to the hotel. But when she got there, she saw many reporters crowding around the front entrance.

"Horrors!" said Miss Mallard aloud. "The news is out about Gadwall's predictions."

ST HOTEL

Miss Mallard squeezed past the reporters and went into the hotel. She saw Officer Pintail and the police chief questioning Gadwall in the lounge.

"I know what I know," Gadwall was saying. "Tomorrow morning at exactly ten o'clock, during the boat races, some of the boats will be destroyed. A riot will break out and the Dragon Boat Festival will end in disaster."

"We must prevent that from happening," said Officer Pintail.

"I'll send a large police force to the races in the morning," said the chief.

Miss Mallard was puzzled. Why did all of Gadwall's predictions involve the police? She excused herself and went to her room. It had been an exhausting day, and she needed to be alone so she could think.

She ordered supper in her room. All evening she went over the events of the day. But at bedtime she was still as puzzled as ever.

Miss Mallard thought about her only clue, the gray thread, which she had placed in her travel guidebook. She opened the book. The thread was still there. She closed the book again and stared at it. Then she put it away and went to sleep.

When Miss Mallard awoke the next morning, it was already nine o'clock. And Gadwall's prediction was set for ten!

Miss Mallard bounded out of bed. And suddenly everything was clear to her! She grabbed her knitting bag. She reached inside and gave her travel guide a pat. Then she dug through her clipping file for a particular news item.

"Zounds!" she said when she found it.

Quickly, she got dressed and ran to the front desk. She asked where she could find the Gadwalls.

"Sorry," said the clerk. "They checked out this morning."

"I thought so!" said Miss Mallard.

She rushed outside.

"Quick!" she cried to Lee Long Duck. "Take me to Officer Pintail."

When they found Officer Pintail, Miss Mallard said, “It’s about the Gadwalls! They left the hotel! Right at this moment I believe that they are stealing the million-dollar jade necklace that is on display at the Duckworth Museum! The accident and predictions were faked! The Gadwalls planned to keep the police busy so the museum would be less protected against robbery!”

“Great Dragons!” said Officer Pintail. “I’ll send a police car to the museum right away!”

Lee Long Duck sped with Miss Mallard to the museum. Officer Pintail and the other police were already there. They were crowded around the museum's side entrance.

Miss Mallard went over. She saw Marshall Gadwall, Melissa Gadwall, and Harold, all in handcuffs.

"Well, you were right, Miss Mallard," said Officer Pintail. "We caught them in the act, just as they were coming out the door with the necklace."

"How did you know we would be here?" grumbled Marshall Gadwall.

“Thanks to my guidebook,” said Miss Mallard. “I saw a picture of the jade necklace in it, and I remembered that your wife said she was ‘shopping’ for jade. I also remembered that you said you were a retired navy captain. Since when do navy captains get seasick on floating restaurants? Then all it took was a look in my clipping file to find out your true identity—‘Slippery’ Gadwall, the well-known thief and swindler.”

Miss Mallard paused and reached into her knitting bag. She pulled out the gray thread.

HONG

"Here is a thread that I found at the floating restaurant," said Miss Mallard. "As you can see, it matches Harold's jacket. Not only that, you claimed that your wife had gone shopping yesterday morning. And yet she returned to the hotel empty-handed. I believe that you sent your wife and Harold out to cause the events that you 'predicted.' And you followed me to fake the rickshaw accident, knowing that I would get the police involved. It was all a scheme to fool the police, so the museum would be less protected while you robbed it."

"Take them away," said Officer Pintail to the squad. "I'll tell the chief that there will be no trouble at the Dragon Boat Races."

Then Officer Pintail turned to Miss Mallard and said, “Good job!”

“Well, I’m glad we saved the necklace,” said Miss Mallard. “The Gadwalls had me fooled for a while.”

Lee Long Duck said, “How about seeing the sights of Hong Kong now—very slowly?”

“Why, Lee Long!” said Miss Mallard. “What a good idea!”